# THE PROUD

## AND THE IMMORTAL

# THE PROUD
## AND THE IMMORTAL

**Oswald Rivera**

Polar Bear & Company
Solon Maine U.S.A.
www.polarbearandco.com

Polar Bear & Company
P.O. Box 311, Solon, Maine 04979 U.S.A.
207 643-2795
polarbear@skow.net
www.polarbearandco.com

Cover design by Emily du Houx. Cover photo by Paul Goldstein.
First edition, 2003. Manufactured in the U.S.A.
by Thomson-Shore, Inc., an employee owned company.
Library of Congress Control Number 2003107910
ISBN 1-882190-74-2

And they said, Go to, let us build us
a city and a tower, whose top [may
reach] unto heaven; and let us make us
a name, lest we be scattered abroad
upon the face of the whole earth.
Genesis 11:4

# Foreword

As university students taking part in various community service programs, we have observed the inner workings of this shared catastrophe and spent significant time working hands-on with individuals afflicted by hunger, poverty and homelessness. We have been fortunate to be a part of many comprehensive experiences in shelters and soup kitchens and have enjoyed engaging in encounters with the many remarkable people who live in poverty in New York City. Our study in service is a process that combines knowledge of the facts profiling the homeless dilemma with a larger depth of understanding gained through exposure to the fundamental humanity we all share as citizens of a nation. Ultimately, this service need not be a matter of what 'we' (the privileged) can offer 'them' (the underprivileged) but a matter of relating to people as people and using our collective ideas, choices and perspectives to educate ourselves and those around us on a multifaceted problem which correlates strongly with our multifaceted society. Furthermore, it is important to emphasize that this is indeed a society that belongs to all of us. It is *our* problem; our education will bring understanding, our understanding will facilitate a solution.

In developing this process we must call for resources. We will require educational tools by which every person, despite class, race or gender, will come to an equitable and informed understanding of the systems in which we are a part. Oswald Rivera's book is indispensable as one of these resources. Simply put, Mr. Rivera sheds humanistic light on the homeless condition. *The Proud and the Immortal* is a stepping stone on a path towards the education of our country on the crisis of homelessness. His book is the voice for a culture of real people in real need. Rivera has written an informative and honest novel that depicts the fundamental realities of the vulnerability to the outer world, strength from the inner world, and the constant courage that encompasses the lives of the downtrodden and homeless.

For those of us in comparatively privileged economic—albeit middleclass—situations, it is easy to focus on the financial struggles presented to us as standard expectations of America's working population (i.e. college, career, children, property, cars, etc.) It is in turn just as easy to feel that we should not be held accountable for the mistakes and misfortunes of others and it is therefore not our duty to cope with the suffering we live amidst.

The crisis of homelessness in our nation is a growing issue of which many of us are often misinformed and unaware. Homelessness and its role in the United States is not getting as much attention and examination as its severity warrants. Its trend is undeniably widespread. We are accustomed to the presence of a homeless faction and have become desensitized to the sights of homeless and hungry people. What we may not realize, however, is the seriousness of this rising social calamity and the extent to which it exists. It is a crisis of sociological, as well as political, concern. The lack of resources available to those living in destitution is enabled by a society that, in its structure, is ill-equipped to facilitate change.

For the homeless individual the challenge of rising out of poverty and homelessness is a lengthy, complex and arduous process. In our research of statistics we have found that in no state does a full-time minimum-wage job cover the costs of a one-bedroom unit at Fair Market Rent. In addition to this, it is also known that families make up 78 percent of New York City's homeless shelter population. More than one in four children in the city currently lives in poverty, a typical homeless child being under the age of five. It is easy to see that in many cases, and especially for children or other unemployable persons, even the imminent solutions offered by state and traditional social service programs are temporary and inadequate. Other proposed solutions for long-term prevention of homelessness and hunger often do not manifest due to lack of funding and support. Though over 38,000 homeless individuals in New York City use the city's shelter system each day, and thousands more hungry people receive their daily meals from soup kitchens and food pantries, every day these establishments collectively turn away over 2,500 people.

In a country built and based on doctrines of prosperity, freedom and equality, the realities of homelessness may be a bitter pill to swallow for the politically powerful. However, the hard truth remains that homeless people are, by majority, unable to enjoy or even experience the fundamental American freedoms of speech, religion, freedom from fear, and freedom from want.

Dylan Fuller & Zoey Foster

All statistics from: The National Coalition for the Homeless, updated May 2003; New York Times, 2002; Hunger Action Network of New York State, 1999; New York City Coalition Against Hunger, 1998.

# PROLOGUE

W HEN SHE HEARD THEM coming the first time, it was from far away. Then the footsteps got heavier as they came nearer. She knew instinctively she had to get out. Like she always did, ever since she could recall, as far back as her mind would let her, even back before everything had changed into a hazy non-remembrance. What she could remember was immediate; all those other thoughts and more recent memories meshed in the portion of her mind where nothing surfaced and all was confusion. But now the voice told her to run. She had no fear, no anxiety, just hunger and thirst and the need to pee and the need to move. But this was different.

She roused herself, trying to get up from the old mattress inside the tunnel. A secure place, especially when she needed to get away from the others in the caverns above. For the others were like her; they drifted, most with dead stares that felt nothing and too much. And they all joined together in a babble of words, many of which she could never know or possibly imagine.

She raised her head, feeling vaguely ill, and tired. Muscle bone tired. Slowly, she turned one bleak eye to beyond the entrance of the tunnel, where the ceilings dripped brackish water with a constant regularity. Where the mini-puddles formed and dead rats floated placidly on their sides, after Horse had killed them with a lead pipe and a good shot to the head. To be cannibalized by other colonies of rats whom Horse, in his quest, had not yet slain with his time-honored method.

She surveyed the overhead pipes that connected to form a cross above the dark void that led to the second level. The air was dense. It saturated the mattress and seeped into her shoes and thick tights. The cotton in her drawers had caked to form a second skin bound and glued by unaccounted feces and menstrual flow, all of it anchored by a hot, stinging dampness borne by steam and tubing. A dampness that preserved not only moisture, but her own odor of decay. But these were not considerations, by her lights. Her understanding was based on sense and need. Undefined cravings, to carry and lug about what she deemed important, in that corner of her mind where the ghost of reason prevailed.

Hoarse whispers and heavy breathing. She arched her head, trying to listen. Nothing came back at her. She extended one scrawny hand to set it firmly on the floor, lifting her body to a crouching position, and finally to her feet, half standing, half bent, with a thread of drool that slid down her chin to settle on the first button of her faded cardigan. She had exactly three bags of possessions. Light travel in her frame of mind. At one time there had been many more, plus a shopping cart, plus an old leather suitcase, and a ripped golf bag—where she found it, she couldn't recall. All the possessions just seemed to appear.

"We gotta hurry, man. C'mon, we gotta hurry!"

In between the whispers, more footfalls. Akin to three separate horses on a racetrack, one going slowly and two going fast. A recollection of a long-ago time in a country field. She saw the racetrack again. The grooms currying the fillies and thoroughbreds. The smell of hay and easily raked dirt that became a quagmire in the rains. There was a man, of slight build, with heavy sinewy arms and caramel skin. A man who looked just like her.

"They gotta be round here, c'mon."

They were almost at the outer rim of the tunnel, very near to the last burrow where she had lived for the past two weeks, before the massive rains had poured into the top ledges, seeping into the concrete gratings and air shafts. With effort, she grasped one bag with her right hand and clawed the other two in her left. Then she moved out in a shambling gait that evolved through no conscious effort but that had become as much a part of her as the tattered belongings in her brain.

The listless shuffle took her about two yards from where she had lain. Here the tunnel came to a dead end. Though this was not its actual end. The tunnel was a continuous maze, circumventing the city's innards. Where a dead end came, invariably another exit was found, and then another until it ended nowhere, for no one had yet surveyed its distance. The tunnels would go on forever: subway tunnels, bridge tunnels, housing tunnels and project tunnels, underground lanes and construction holes, all seemingly interconnected, if not by fact, then by her mind, since they all joined somehow. An amorphous spider's web with the center being her belongings, whatever she could scavenge or carry. Items that became so precious they were soon forgotten.

She reached an adjoining wall that led to the near exit and round a corner, coming upon a smaller enclosure which was darker and narrower. One of the many stagnant puddles had formed about three feet from the enclosure wall. Slowly, with measured steps, she avoided the puddle, gently kicking aside a plastic soda bottle. She studiously avoided getting her feet wet. The flat pumps that she wore had been found in the rocklike outcroppings where the others stayed. She had searched the inner passageways, only to stumble upon the shoes, which to her had become a treasure. Shiny and black, pointed and open toed. She couldn't consider getting them wet—especially when something had moved in the water. She jumped back, startled. Her breath caught, but she managed to suppress the gasp that could have been be heard down the line.

Leaning forward, she peered into the dark, sensing a non-light separating from the near-light of the exit. Water in the puddle glistened as if streaked by invisible moonlight. She cocked her head to one side, straining to hear whatever it was in the puddle. No sound. Though something had scampered back to the exit. Still straining to hear, coming up empty. Now she considered that, maybe, just maybe, she had heard nothing. It had happened before... Just as quickly, the sounds caught her again: "They gotta be somewheres, man, they gotta be..."

She skirted the edge of the puddle, ambling along the tunnel wall. The smell of the fetid water followed her inch by inch.

She reached the spot where the wall opened into a smaller cave. Here asbestos-wrapped tubing flanged upward to be lost in a welter of narrow pipes that shrouded whatever light trickled from above. She lowered to her knees, and began to shove her belongings into the smaller cave. When the bags were hidden, she crept inside on all fours, dragging her overcoat along the edge where the tunnel floor met the wall, the coat rubbing ever so gently on rodent droppings. The smell,

if tepid outside, was insufferable inside this hollow. The odor of shit
had long been replaced by a stronger mix of urine, rotting food and
used tampons. At one time this tunnel annex had served as the
communal privy—until she claimed it as her domain.

Once inside the hole, she pressed back against the three bags,
crouching further within the narrow confines. She squinted into the
outer shaft that led back to the main tunnel, saw nothing. She was
inside a cocoon as closed as her mind. Paramount to her nature was
the yen to push her being so far into itself that she'd never need come
out. She would remain forever in the shade of that long ago racetrack
on a sultry summer afternoon with a sinewy black man grooming a
chestnut mare.

An arm lifted in the dark, near her face. She realized it was her
own. She peered at her hand, feeling the fingers spread out in dim
outlines. She tried to make out the color, that caramel tinge which was
so different from the deep hue of Ratman whose skin resembled
Pennsylvania coal, or from the light brown of Lucho. Or the sallow
whiteness of the woman called Olga and the old man with the breath
of the dying. She recalled that her skin had once been smooth, like
onyx; and she remembered other colors and other skin: ocher, cocoa,
tawny, coffee colored, and large hands, many hands clapping, and big
white teeth hollering and singing... and it had been so hot inside the
chapel, almost as hot as inside the tunnel, but not as wet, nor as dark,
but just as loud with a shrill that rose and died to a bare minimal
whisper that said: "They gotta be here—they's gotta be!"

"But this crazy, man—ain't no one here..."

They were all around! Different voices clamoring inside her head.
She shrank deeper into the cave, feeling the odds and ends of her
bags jabbing into her spine. Sweat streaked her forehead and cheeks.
There was the stickiness of the sweater beneath the work shirt beneath
the coat she wore summer and winter. Only her feet with the open-
toe pumps felt dry. The rest of her was soaked.

A sliver of grayish light filtered into the tunnel from the outside.
This, in turn, compressed into a small rectangular shaft of light, about
a foot or so. On impulse, she crawled forward, scraping her elbows
and shins on the dried waste hardened into pebbles. The sliver of

light enlarged as she crept nearer the exit. This led her to the lip of the cave which was shaded by part of a slanting concrete wall which hid the entrance so that she could observe the outer cave without being seen.

Outside, the three men continued a restless search on unknown territory. They all dressed the same, she realized suddenly. Identical running shoes and baggy jeans, with gray T-shirts showing some lettering which she couldn't know. Once she could make out certain words, but she had forgotten how. Yet her feeble wits could discern that they were young, or appeared to be young. With black hair and dark skin and dirty sneakers rubbing on concrete, making squirrel-like noises only she could hear.

One of them had a mustache. Pencil thin, similar to peach fuzz that refuses to grow. His hair at the sides was close-cropped, with shaven lines on his skull, and his left ear showed an earring. His accomplices had similar hair except that the lines etched into their skulls were diagonal or crisscrossed. But only the mustachioed one carried the large metal can with the dark stained spout. He clutched the can so tightly that a small nerve pulsed on the right side of his face just above the jaw bone.

"They ain't nuttin' here, Indio," one of the youths said. His voice was thin, uncertain. He looked younger than his two companions, and worried.

"No, man, there somp'n here," the one with the mustache replied. They couldn't gotten away."

"This a fucken dead end, man."

Pencil-mustache shook his head, his eyes darting from one corner to the other. "Someone gotta be here. No place they can go."

"Wha-wha-we do-do-do-now?" the third one said haltingly, as if the effort in forming the words was more taxing than any physical exertion.

"We search," pencil-mustache decided.

"But where, man?" the thin one asked.

The one with the mustache cradled the can as if it were gold. "Anywhere, *everywhere,* I don't give a fuck. We gotta find one that's all."

In the safety of the inner chamber, the rodent had trekked a familiar pathway. Long exposure to two-legged creatures had honed his instincts even though he had only three legs. But they gave him enough momentum to scramble through the faulty pipes and leap out of the crevice above the woman with the smell of the tunnels. The rat made a three point landing on her shoulder; it's elongated snout scraped her left cheek, and she screeched.

Immediately she clamped a hand to her mouth; but it came up, from deep in her stomach. A loud gurgle rumbled from the back of her tongue.

To the men in the outer cave it roared as a groan amplified by the outer cave wall. A groan that ended in a howl.

The one with the thin voice was the first to glance at the slanting wall shielding the smaller cave. His friend with the stutter followed his gaze where a faint croak hung suspended inside the grotto—where she clutched her throat, trying to hold down whatever was coming up. She coughed lightly, swallowed hard, feeling something stuck between her mouth and belly.

The one with the stutter was taller and stockier than the others, with a massive bull's neck joining the width of his shoulders. He lumbered to the slanting wall. "Wha-wha-wha-what..." The stutter held him fast.

"We got 'im!" Pencil-mustache dropped to one knee in front of the triangle formed by the slanting wall.

The one with the thin voice knelt right behind him. "What is it?"

Pencil-mustache gestured with the can to where the shadows hid the cave. "It came from there!"

The hacking rose again. Too late to push back the humors that had gone from a mere trickle to a fist grasping her windpipe. She heard someone coughing in the distance... and knew it was her. She sniffled, wiping her nose with the back of her hand, and huddled inside.

Pencil-mustache craned his neck until it edged past the crevice made by the curving wall. His face and neck dissolved in the shadows while his lower torso remained in the dying light of the outer cave.

"What you see, man?" the one with the thin voice asked. "What you see?"

Pencil-mustache crawled on one knee, pushing forward with his elbows.

She sensed the presence inside her cave and she drew back further—coming up against a barrier wall. With one quick movement she brought her knees up to her chest. The heavy coat scratched her thighs.

"Where are ya, you fucker?" pencil-mustache called to the blackness.

She gulped, fighting the pressure in her throat.

"I know you there."

She twisted sideways, with the legs still jammed against her chest.

The man squirmed inside the hollow, his arm brushing against something hard yet moist. A pungent odor flecked his nose. With one hand he swept away whatever littered his path. A vain attempt to wipe clean his jeans and T-shirt only served to smear his hands and wrists. "Shit!" he yelled to the others outside. "This place is fulla shit!"

"What the fuck d'ya want?" came the response from thin-voice. "Tole ya this place was a hellhole..."

"Fuck," pencil-mustache muttered. "Gimme a light."

"Whut?"

Pencil-mustache slapped at his legs, trying to remove the crud from his clothing. "Gimme a light."

The younger man jammed his hands inside his pants pocket and took out a Bic lighter. The flame it gave illuminated just enough of the cave so that he could see his friend's sneakers as they stuck out of the inner chamber.

"Can't see shit," the leader said from inside. "Throw the light over here."

Thin-voice glanced uncertainly at the small flame in his hand. He blew out the light and tossed the plastic lighter inside.

"Where d'fuck is it?" growled the one inside the cave.

"I threw it by yore legs," thin-voice said.

"Where?"

"By yore legs, man—by yore feet."

"Can't see nuttin'."

"Look fer it, man."

Pencil-mustache extended his hand and patted the floor. Shards of waste dug into his palm. "Coño... carajo..."

"Look fer it, man... look fer it..."

The one inside pounded the floor with the bottom of his fist.

Then his elbow brushed something jagged. He turned on his side, scanning the ground with his left hand and finding the lighter. A flick of his thumb and a sphere of light bounced on the interior wall. Everywhere he looked there was feces. "Fuck!"

"What is it, man?" his friend asked from the outside.

"This place is a shithole, man," he shot back. "A fucken shithole."

The light touched the open-toe pumps; then it revealed the ballerina tights, pukey brown in color. Pencil-mustache was startled. He had chased the prey but hadn't expected a pair of disembodied feet covered in brown stockings. More strange, the feet didn't move. They just remained there, inert. He extended his arm and the radius of light encompassed a tattered winter coat, and part of a leathery brown face. The uneven features were ghastly: a small prune atop a mound of clothing. "Goddam..."

"Whut?"

Pencil-mustache didn't reply. Instead, holding tight to the Bic lighter, he flicked his hand at the woman's face. She flinched, shielding her face with her arms.

The man tried to rise on his knees but his rump hit the wall above him. "Goddam."

He lunged at her, his T-shirt and pants gliding on the turds beneath him. He was now close enough to make a grab for her feet. But she pulled back, and he found himself desperately trying to steady his hand with the tiny light whirling in the dark.

She was more than a veteran of the tunnels. Sometimes her mind would trick her, and sometimes her bearings took hold. So she quickly rolled away in the cramped space, flattening a generation of human waste with her winter coat, moving away from the near wall and coming flat against another wall. She sniffed her way down the wall to floor level. The stench of dried feces was replaced by that of putrid wood. She tightened one hand into a fist and jammed it into the wooden planks near the floor. The wood snapped. Moisture combined with age had given it the consistency of cardboard.

Two pieces of rotted wood blocked her way. She grasped one of the beams and pushed it down so that a small opening appeared, no bigger than her shoulders. But wide enough to accommodate her bulk as she passed from one tunnel into another.

The man behind her snapped at her heels with his hand holding the lighter which fluttered uncertainly. And finally snuffed out.

"Shit." Anger replaced frustration. Putting his body in reverse, he began crawling backward, lifting his hands off the floor as much as the meager space would allow. In a matter of seconds he made it back to where the large can lay waiting.

His younger companion trembled with nervous energy. "You find 'im?"

"There's a bitch in there."

"Whut?"

"There's some old bitch in there," pencil-mustache said quickly.

"I thought it was a some dude we wuz chasin'?"

Pencil-mustache nodded toward the inner chamber. "No, man, there's some old bitch in there 'n we gonna get 'er." He picked up the can.

Thin-voice exhaled. "Coño."

The stockier man had remained standing at the entryway. He regarded his friend and the metal can with a look of anticipation. "Who-who."

Pencil-mustache heaved the can outward, splashing the reeking liquid inside the smaller cave.

The younger one pivoted to the side, yelling, "Be careful, man, you gonna get that stuff on me!"

Pencil-mustache swung the can to and fro, saturating the hole. He planted the can on the ground and looked about for the miniature lighter. Realizing he had lost it, he quickly searched his pockets, extracting a book of matches. He lit a match, then the matchbook and, with a flick of the wrist, tossed the matchbook inside the cave.

The gasoline flared in small tendrils that blossomed into a searing ball. The men in the outer cave jumped back from the pincers licking the tunnel walls.

Inside, she scuttled beyond the exit she had made and into a large drainage pipe. She threw a glance over her shoulder, feeling the scorching air fluttering near her feet. The ball of flame expanded into the exit; fiery coils threaded their way past the wooden beams.

Fighting for breath, she scrambled beyond the drainpipe, coming upon another, but larger extension to the tunnel, where she got to her feet and turned another corner in the cavern.

And stopping dead in her tracks when she found herself facing the main tunnel, and not twenty feet from where the three youths stood staring at the fire crackling inside the smaller chamber. The maze had led her right back to square one.

She moved back two steps, ducking behind the retaining wall facing the outer cave. With a short, silent breath, she flattened her body against the concrete. She closed her eyes, feeling a pounding in her breastbone.

Thin-voice tugged at pencil-mustache's arm. "Let's go, man. Let's go!"

From behind the retaining wall, she sought to keep down the acids percolating on her tongue. The dank odor of her threadbare sleeve rose to her nose, momentarily masking the taste of vomit. The cave was consumed with a charred smell. She thought of fat on an open fire and retched. The smell of seared wood mingled with that of scorched cement.

She scooted out of the tunnel, moving as fast as she could in her awkward stride, out toward the upper caverns and the street, to warn the others.

# BOOK ONE

## HOME

**I**

Murphy first saw him loitering about the Häagen Dazs concession wedged in between the refreshment bar and the Dunkin' Donuts shop. Worn out but defiant. The guy exhibited the same vacuous stare as the rest of them, with his hands deep in his pockets, even though it was high summer, and the air in the station was hellish. No one paid him much attention, since they came and went, all of those like him, stepping alone, ignoring the staid commuters huffing to catch the next express. He was of slight build, with dark complexion and curly brown hair badly in need of trimming. Also, he hadn't shaved in a couple of days. But more, this new blood walked as if wound tight in the gut. And the tightness increased as he cased the bins which stored the eight varieties of ice cream readily available to the public in single and double scoops, sugar-cone or regular.

Yet the kid eyed the bins, not with the yearning of the hungry, but with the resignation of someone who knew he could never again afford what the bins supplied, and who took it with a grudging acceptance, while behind the counter the hefty Puerto Rican girl in the green smock and white hat brim gave him a look of hardy suspicion. The way those who thought they had something always regarded those who they thought had nothing.

The youth glared back at the proper Rican waitress. She looked away. So he sauntered out to the main thoroughfare, stopping to peruse the various window displays and getting in return the stare of the unwelcome. Finally he stopped at the newsstand next to the takeout pizza parlor.

At the newsstand he got the same guarded look from the Bengali part owner who stood behind rows of candy bars and junk food. The youth surveyed the numerous magazines with all their illustrations. Then gazed briefly at the Bengali part owner, his face shooting back the same antipathy it received.

Next, the new blood moved on to stop in front of a picture-frame shop which displayed a portable notebook computer with a framed sign: NOTHING LIKE IT FOR THE EXEC ON THE GO. For a moment he scanned the black-bordered sign above the shop.

The young man then locked his eyes to the distance, as if distracted. Murphy knew what he was thinking: "Where is my next meal coming from?" That, or, "Where is my next high coming from?" Though Murphy suspected this turkey wasn't one of the crackerjacks.

Murphy reached down for the half pint of Night Train wrapped nice and safe in the brown bag. He took a sip and placed the bag upright against the wall where he sat with his legs bent and his arms draped over his knees.

The wine flushed his empty stomach with a false warmth, producing a loathsome gas which had long ceased to bother anyone in his group. The smell of their clothing was probably more potent than any of his grubby farts.

Now he heard a familiar entreaty: "Murphy, friend, what say you give a sip, huh?" The rummy known as Old Luther held out his hand in a supplicating gesture. "What say, Murphy? Jus' a sip?"

Murphy scowled, turning his head. "Git away."

Old Luther gave a long sigh, and moved on with his hand still outstretched like a beacon.

Once more Murphy turned his attention to the new blood who had bumped into a fat man in a seersucker suit and requisite attaché case. The big-bellied man, sweating miserably in the foul air, didn't have a chance to sidestep the disheveled stranger standing in his way. He muttered something to the new blood, perhaps a "pardon me" or such. But the new blood, a hard case indeed, responded with a look of pure hate.

The commuter did not back down. He outweighed the skinny vagrant by about 50 pounds, so perhaps he wasn't worried. "You should watch where you're going." Murphy heard the fat man gripe in a loud voice.

"An' you should shove that case up yore ass," the hard case snarled, jutting out his lower lip and hooking his thumbs in his back pockets just like they did back on the block. Except this wasn't the block, and here one didn't ride on bravado alone.

The fat commuter did not take up the challenge. He sized up the vagrant with no more regard than one would an insect. Then he hunched his shoulders inside the seersucker suit and continued on his way.

The hard case glared at the retreating back of the empty suit. But he didn't move. Finally showing some sense, Murphy said to himself. He had learned long ago that in run-ins with commuters, the street folks always came out losing, even when they won. And they never won.

The hard case resumed his stroll toward the other side of the station, exactly for the spot where Murphy knew he would end up. He shoved aside the flattened cardboard box that belonged to Lula and sat down with his back cushioned by the square pillar bulging out of the wall.

Murphy smiled knowingly. Won't Lula be surprised. He took another swallow of Night Train.

The slug of wine hadn't settled in his stomach before he eyed Horse and Lucho coming his way. These two shared a look of anticipation.

It was Lucho who began in his raspy voice: "Who that doofus in Lula's spot? That dude jus' askin' to get hurt."

"I know," Murphy replied, keeping his eye on the hard case.

Horse put down the trash bag full of empty beer cans and soda bottles that he carried over his shoulder. "Ever see 'im b'fore?" he asked.

"Nope," Murphy said. "Never seen 'im before."

Horse put a hand to his forehead, pushing forward the sock-like cap he wore year round. "Somebody better tell 'im to skip," he stated. "If Lula catch 'im in her spot, his ass is grass."

Lucho scratched his chin, giving Murphy a sheepish look. "By the way, Murphy, iffen you got some t' spare I wouldn't mind a sip." He gestured to the pint bottle inside the brown bag, and smiled disarmingly. Unlike Murphy, he had all his teeth, still perfectly even. Which bothered Murphy. He had always considered that at the rate Lucho hit the cheap muscatel he should have lost his teeth and gums, along with his liver, long ago. Yet he remained the same: squat but wiry, with a checkered cap that concealed woolly sideburns that came down to his cheekbones. All of it hooked together by heavy-lidded eyes that gave him the air of perpetually being stoned, even when sober.

"What happened to the pint from last night?" Murphy asked.

"We met some homeboys," Lucho said. "So we shared. Y'know how it is."

Murphy smiled, showing a missing front tooth. "Yeah, I know how it is." Before he could offer Lucho a drink, he saw Lula who approached in rapid stride. She aped the swivel-hip gait common to the street folk. In one hand she carried a small red handbag which she held in full view, almost daring anyone, fish or mugger, to snatch the purse. "Oh, boy," Murphy breathed.

Horse caught site of her as well. "Oh, oh."

"Who da fuck is that motherfucker settin' in my spot?" Lula snarled when she was within hearing distance.

Horse shrugged. "Dunno."

Lula turned to Lucho. "You know who dat fucker is?"

Lucho gazed nonchalantly at the youth sitting in Lula's cherished spot. "Never saw the dude b'fore. Must be new."

"Fucking no shit, Sherlock. That skeezer, however he is, took my spot."

Lucho was nonplused. "So?"

"*So?*" Lula's eyes' widened. "What da fuck you assholes gonna do 'bout it?"

"Whatcha mean, what *we* gonna do 'bout it—it's yore spot."

"Nigger, cain't you see that fucker took my spot?"

Horse sighed and offered reasonably, "Mebbee he don't know it's your spot."

Lula shot him a quick glance and said, "That make no motherfucken dif'rence. It still my fucken spot 'n he settin' in it."

Murphy eyed Lula with detached amusement. "Ask 'im to move," he suggested.

"Yore right," she said, seething. "That's what I'm gonna fucken do right now."

She took off, with a determined set to her jaw, heading directly for the hard case.

"We better go with 'er," Horse warned. "Y'know how steamed up she can git." He glanced at the young man on the other side. "He look just about as pissed as she does. This could get mean."

"Yup," Murphy said, standing up and shoving the half pint into his back pocket.

They caught up with Lula who, arms akimbo, stared down at the unkempt new blood. She leveled a finger at him and demanded, "You, skeezer, out!" She flicked her thumb over her shoulder.

The hard case raised his eyebrows, surprised. "What?"

"You settin' in my fucken spot," Lula snapped.

The hard case drew his eyebrows together. "I din't see no sign here sez it's your spot."

"Well, it fucken is."

The youth said in an even voice: "Look, lady, I don't wanna fuck with nobody. So don't fuck with me."

Lula spoke to Lucho and Horse, who stood directly behind her. "You see this here fucker? He don't want nobody to fuck with 'im." Then at the youth: "I bet you ain't movin' either, right?"

The youth clasped his hands together, showing a deliberate tension. "Don't fuck with me, lady."

"You gonna move or am I gonna hafta kick yore butt outta there?" Lula threatened.

Before the man was halfway up, with his legs still bent beneath him, Lucho and Horse had clamped a hand on each shoulder, pushing his back against the wall. "You heard the lady," Horse said curtly. "You in her spot."

The youth lurched forward. The two men shoved him back. He brought a fist up to his chest. But Lucho grabbed the hand, pinning the arm to the wall. Horse let go of the trash bag and was about to let him have it right in the throat when he heard Murphy from behind: "Let 'im go."

Lucho and horse kept pressing on the young man.

"I said, let 'im go," Murphy ordered.

Lucho did not take his eyes off the youth. "He a hard-on, Murph," he muttered. "Fucker needs some learnin'."

Right on cue, the hard-on shot back: "You gonna learn me somp'n?"

Lucho jammed his elbow under the young man's throat.

Murphy placed a hand on Lucho's collarbone. "I said, let 'im go."

Lucho glanced over his shoulder at Murphy, who retained the grip on his clavicle. Frowning, he released his elbow from under the young man's chin. He asked Murphy, "You know this bozo?"

Murphy shook his head. "No. But in another minute we'd all be in the shit." He tilted his head in the direction of the two uniformed policemen who happened to be strolling by.

Horse quickly removed his hand from the youth's shoulder.

Even Lula idly scanned the ground, showing bored unconcern.

When the policemen had passed, Lucho grabbed the young man's arm. "If you wanna keep breathin' you best tip, motherfucker," he growled.

"And if I don't?"

"Then we gonna carry you out," Horse said evenly, *"in pieces."*

The young man reddened. "Who the fuck you think you—"

"You best lissen, young blood," Murphy said in a low cold voice.

The youth met Murphy's eyes. A dull gray-green, with a dark tinge around the irises. When he spoke it was the missing front tooth that caught the youth's attention.

"We ain't gonna tell you twice," Murphy said in that low cold voice. "Y'know?"

"Let me whoop on this fucker," Lucho demanded, "he needs it."

Murphy yanked the bottle from his back pocket and offered it to Lucho. "Here, my man, have a sip." He smiled thinly and added, "Fucker ain't worth a whoopin'."

"Aaaag." Lucho took the wine and downed a snort. He wiped his lips with the back of his hand. "You lucky, dude, y'know that? You jus' be careful, man, where you sit in the future. You may have no ass left to sit with."

The youth was boiling, but he said nothing.

Murphy turned to Lula who was suddenly uncharacteristically quiet. "I believe this gentleman is going to give you back your spot, Lula." Then to the young man, "Ain't that so, bro?"

The youth measured the three in turn. He took a breath, exhaled. Slowly he stepped away from the wall and, as he turned to leave, Murphy said to him, "Hey, what's your name?"

"Who wants to know?"

"Nobody in particular."

The youth didn't respond, and simply walked away, heading to the other side of the station.

"That motherfucker ain't gonna last long here," Lula predicted, taking in the hip-roll walk of the hard case as he receded into the crowd. "He got a bad case of the asses."

"That he do," Murphy concurred. "That he do."

"Asshole's a jackleg," Lucho said, offering the bottle to Horse who took a swig. Horse looked down at the trash bag resting at his feet. "What we gonna do for breakfast?" he asked Lucho. "Wanna scoop more?"

Lucho surveyed the haul. "Nah, we got enuff for a coupla burgers. Besides, Ratman and Ruben should be by wit' their usual load. We can scoop off them."

"If I know them fuckers," Lula said, "they's prob'ly got two cartloads full. They wuz out all night."

Murphy took the bottle from Horse. He was ready to go.

"Where you headed?" Lucho asked him.

"Gonna try and find Gertie."

"Why?" Lula wanted to know. "She'll prob'ly be along. She always come back."

Murphy took a final pull from the pint bottle and capped it closed. "I know, but if what went down last night is true, and she was attacked by some hotbloods, I wanna make sure she with us, not being assaulted by someone who wants to set fire to the tunnels."

"You think that really happened?" Lula asked.

"Hey, we saw the scorch marks on the wall. These guys could be back. A lot goes on in the tunnels. I wish she was here this morning. Don't feel too good with her out in the streets—especially if some dudes are after her."

Lucho was skeptical. "Oh, man, nuttin' gonna happen. She prob'ly didn't see shit. Y'know how she is." He pointed to his temple. "She all scrambled eggs, man."

Murphy sucked thoughtfully at his lower lip. "Scrambled eggs or not, fact is we gotta find Gertie."

Lucho spoke to Horse. "When d'ya think Ratman gonna show?"

"Don't know, man," Horse said. "Could be now, could be later. You hungry?"

"Yeah."

"I could use some grit too," Lula said.

Murphy palmed the bottle, and again turned to leave. "Tell you what, Murphy," Horse told him, "we'll walk you to the dumpster. It's on the way to the McDonald's."

"Suit yourself." Murphy headed for the station escalators, tossing the empty bottle into an overflowing trash bin.

**II**

THEY EMERGED ON THE outside walkway in back of Madison Square Garden. Once outdoors, Lula led the way, skirting a fence to a construction site littering the rear of the building. Alongside the fence stood a large flatbed dump truck filled with discarded refuse which some of the street folk were already scavenging for usable goods. But their interest was sparked not by the dumpster, but by that same young man they had confronted back in the station. The youth was double-timing to the end of the street, as if chasing someone. They looked at each other. Then it hit them all at once and they dashed across the street.

About four yards out, a group of children, perhaps eleven to twelve years old, were lobbing missiles at the weird lady with the funny walk. The youngsters, eight to ten in number, exhibited the mark of their class: snappy blue blazers with the exclusive private school emblem and matching gray slacks. Each carried a blue, vinyl backpack with black straps. They cackled as they heaved the small stones readily picked up from the pavement. The woman dodged the stones in such a lumbering hysterical way that it was hilarious to the privately schooled gents. Funnier than any Nintendo game, especially when she twittered every time a rock struck a limb.

"Hey, stop that!" the hard case hollered.

The young scions froze. It was a momentary surprise. One of the kids hurled a rock at the good Samaritan, who ducked, the stone flying over his head. The man stopped in mid-stride, swept up a fragment of concrete and flung it in their direction.

One of the young scions dropped the rock in his hand, turned and hightailed out of the area. The others were left with scared looks on their faces.

The man picked up another piece of concrete, ready to let go at the lads. From across the street, other worthy citizens came rushing forward: Three men who, even from a distance, reeked of cheap wine and moldy armpits. That wasn't what got the kids, though; it was the woman tagging with them—thin and bony in chino pants, with bruised bronze skin and stringy filaments sticking out of a raccoon scalp. She was yelling every obscenity these pubescent gentlemen had been privy to in the confines of their secluded playgrounds, but not at home. They scattered in every direction.

The young man reached the bag lady first. He started to touch her, but held back. The woman gave off a powerful stench. He retreated two steps, inquiring, "You okay?"

The woman was bunched inside an overcoat, and she stared at him from under her eyebrows. He was taken aback. The eyes didn't match the rest of her. They were young eyes, black and deep set. Yet she gave the appearance of ancient rot.

They weren't alone. The crew that had harassed him in the station now surrounded the woman. They were solicitous in their manner.

Lula took hold of the woman's arm, helped her to straighten up. "You okay, Gertie?"

"They hurt you, Gertie?" he heard the one with the ski cap ask. "You awright?"

"Who were them fuckers?" The second black man wanted to know.

The white man with the missing front tooth came forward and put a hand on Gertie's shoulder. "No broken bones, Gertie?"

She peered at the white man, taking in the familiar face streaked with reddish stubble and a few gray hairs. "Ah's okay, Murphy," she squeaked.

The one called Murphy smiled. "Good. We was worried. You should stick with us, Gertie." He inclined his head in the direction of the street. "It ain't safe out there."

"Ah's knowed dat, Murphy," Gertie stammered. "Jus'... jus' wanned git away... from dem young fellas in da tunnels."

"I don't blame you," Murphy said.

"Them young fuckers topside ain't no better," Lucho asserted.

Lula scoured the ground, taking in the rocks and pebbles strewed about Gertie's feet. "What them fuckers wanna do that for? Pickin' on some woman?" She snapped the air with tight fists. "Iffen I got ahold of one of them doofus, I'd whoop on 'im till he had no ass left."

"It's easy for thems that have, to dump on thems that don't," Horse said. He pushed back the ski cap, revealing a thin scar across his forehead.

The young man stared at the knife wound, then shook free of the image when the white man asked: "You from around here, bro?"

"No, I ain't from around here," the youth replied, with an edge to his voice.

"What's your name?"

The young man didn't answer.

Murphy motioned toward the bag woman. "Look, you tried to help Gertie here, an' we appreciate it. Not many people would have done that."

"Don't like nobody messin' with someone who can't fight back," the young man said tightly.

"My name's Murphy." The white man nodded to the black man with the ski cap, who introduced himself as Horse.

The stocky man with the muttonchops gave a tilt of the head, "I'm Lucho."

Only the black woman with the raccoon hair remained silent.

"You got a place to stay?" Murphy asked.

The youth gave a dour look. "Who wants to know?"

"Just wondering."

The hard case's response was guarded. "Maybe I do, an' maybe I don't."

"We hang out at the station when we ain't scoping out the environment," Murphy told him.

"Nice. Real nice," was all the young man said, and he walked away, heading back across the street.

Lula came alongside Murphy. "He askin' fer it," she said emphatically. "He *really* askin' fer it."

Murphy pinched his lips thoughtfully. "He young. He'll learn."

Lula grimaced. "Not fast enuff to suit me."

"Don't have enuff sense to stay outdoors in this weather," Lucho observed.

"The dude's hungry," Horse guessed. "He prob'ly ain't had a meal in days."

"He do look a bit shitty round the edges," Lula said, "don't he?"

"That he do," Lucho seconded.

Gertie put down her three bags, then slowly straightened, massaging her elbows. "Who wuz dat, Murphy?" Her voice was feeble, like that of a hesitant child.

"Some hard-on, Gertie," Murphy said, looking back at the station entrance. "No one of importance. Just some asshole with a chip on his shoulder."

Lula raised an eyebrow. "More like hammer up his rear."

Murphy gazed at Gertie with concern. "The guys from last night, have you seen 'em again?"

Gertie shook her head from side to side. "Nooo... ain't seen 'em ag'in."

"You sure?"

Gertie moved her head up and down in a slow methodical fashion. "Ah's shore."

Murphy gently took hold of her shoulders. "You gotta be careful. Stick with us and don't say nuthin' to no one, y'understand?"

"Yesss... Ah doo."

"Good. And you go see Olga, y'hear? She worried sick about you."

"Ah knowed..."

"Olga down in the tunnels right now. She tending to the old geezer. You go and help her, y'hear?"

"Ah heah..."

Murphy glanced at Lula. "Can you make sure she get there?"

"No sweat," Lula said.

"Soon as Ratman and Ruben get back with their load, we'll negotiate something and bring you back some grit."

"No problem, Murphy, jus' long as you come back with somp'n."
Lula patted her stomach. "I's starved, man."

"I know. So's we all."

"Let's get goin'," Lucho said impatiently. "Iffen I don't get some
eats soon, I'll drop."

Horse glanced sideways at Lucho. "I doubt that."

"No jivin', man, we gotta get somepin."

Murphy spat to the side. "We will. I suggest we wait for Ratman
and Ruben at the station an' then later on we can hustle for some
coins. Whatcha say?"

"Can't think of nuthin' else to do right now," said Lucho.

Lula tapped lightly on Gertie's coat. "C'mon, honey, let's go back."
She smirked at the others. "Let the *menfolk* do their work."

"Fuck you, Lula," Lucho said good-naturedly.

"Fuck you, too," Lula replied. She led Gertie and her bags across
the street.

Half an hour later Ratman and Ruben appeared bearing the re-
wards of the previous night's foraging. The shopping cart they wheeled
was packed with green and blue trash bags resembling huge balloons
filled with every type of bottle and beer can. To passersby the cart
resembled a giant slug on rollers, with a tumorous growth arising from
its center, almost to a height of six feet.

"Whew!" Horse exclaimed, admiring the haul. "You got some, man."

"Wow," was all Lucho could say.

Murphy surveyed the cart straining beneath the weight of the
garbage bags, and the two men standing proudly alongside. "You guys
busted heavy last night, din'tcha?"

Ratman was first to respond. "Nuttin' to it," he said smugly.

"Oh, come on, mein," his companion complained. "We works berry
hard for dis sheet. Stay up all fockin night. Mucho carajo, joo know?"

Ratman made a deprecatory gesture. "Ahhh, don't lissen to Ruben,
man. He always bitchin'."

Murphy took another gander at the piled-up trash bags. "I don't
know, man. Seeing that load you got, you guys musta hustle."

Ratman began removing the work gloves he always carried on his excursions. "Well, mebbee we did hump a little." He smiled with false modesty.

"Joo mean, hoomp," Ruben put in.

"We *both* hump," Ratman corrected.

Looking at the two men, Murphy could never imagine a more mismatched pair. Ratman was wiry, like Lucho, but without Lucho's small paunch. His skin was a bit darker than Lucho's medium brown. Same blunt features except for a bald spot on the crown of his head. He always wore a stained, cutoff green sweatshirt with a Buffalo Bills logo on it. Ruben was older, and shorter, maybe five feet, with strands of graying hair bushing out of a New York Mets baseball cap. But what struck one immediately were the thick lenses perched on his nose and which magnified his eyeballs to three times their normal size. This was emphasized rather than diminished by the white Zapata mustache set on a lined Iberian face. Whether he could see anything with or without the eyeglasses was open to dispute, though he had an uncanny nose for scavenging anything and everything.

Murphy poked one of the trash bags hanging from the side of the cart. "What time didya start?"

Ratman rubbed the side of his nose. "Oh. 'Bout six or so. We wuz lucky, y'know. We hit the right spots at the right time—dumpsters, bins, rest'rants, you name it."

"You did good."

"We hoomp, mein," Ruben insisted. "We hoomp."

"Can see that," Murphy commented.

"So how we gonna divvy up the rotation?" Ratman wanted to know.

Lucho took stock of the packed empties. "We can make 'nuther trip iffen we can't do it on one try." He nodded to Murphy. "Not bad this rotation jive. Just like the military, right?"

Murphy frowned. "Yeah, just like the military."

Ratman and Ruben didn't waste any time in unloading the heap. They each grabbed three bags; one slung over the shoulder and two clasped in one hand. Murphy followed their lead. "Where's your old lady?" he asked Ruben.

Ruben angled his head back slightly to facilitate the bag draped over his shoulder. "She stay in da shelta. Only way she get bath, she say."

Horse lifted a bag from the cart. "You guys stay in the shelter last night?"

"Shure."

Horse put the bag on the floor, joining it with the two he had hauled all morning. "Why, man? It wuz nice out last night." He gestured at Lucho. "We stay outdoors in the sheep meadow."

"Migda, she no like staying outside," Ruben explained, "not even in temprachure like dis. She pree-fer shelta."

"Even afta what happens in 'em?" Lucho asked.

Ruben grunted. "Das what she say."

"I know how it is, Ruben," Murphy offered. "The street scene can be rough on a family."

"Hell, the street scene can be rough on anyone," Lucho remarked.

"But 'specially on a woman," Horse said.

Lucho pursed his lips in disdain. "Yeah? You wouldn't know that by Lula."

"Lula's a special case, man," was Horse's quick reply. "She can survive anywhere long as she's pissed off."

"When ain't she ever pissed off?" Ratman said dryly.

Murphy had a ready answer. "Maybe that's what makes her strong."

"That's what makes her a pain in the ass," Lucho said, deadpan.

Murphy gave a knowing chuckle. "Yeah, that's true too."

"Fack," Lucho said, "she can be as much of a bitch as Olga sometimes."

"Whatcha mean?" Murphy asked, his voice suddenly testy.

Lucho wet his lips. "Well, Olga can cop a mean attitude iffen we don't bring somp'n back."

"Lady's not a bitch, man," Murphy said. "She just lookin' out for the old guy."

"Yeah, I know," Lucho carped. "It's the old dude that's the bitch."

Murphy's face grew stern. "Look, I told you not to snap on that old dude, he sick an'—"

"We wasting time, mein," Ruben interrupted. "Me hungry too."

Murphy glanced at Lucho momentarily; then he spoke to Ruben. "Yeah, you're right. Let's get this thing done."

Ruben and Ratman wheeled the cart in the opposite direction, bidding Murphy and Lucho a terse, "Later."

When the two were out of sight, Murphy said to Lucho, "You got a mouth on you sometimes, y'know that?"

Lucho feigned surprise. "What's buggin' you, man?"

"Not all women are bitches, y'know."

Lucho regarded Murphy for a moment. "Oh, so we's pissed off now, huh?"

"You don't get it, do you?"

"Get what? Olga's jus' a street broad, man. Ain't no dif'rent from any of us."

"Look, just because a woman has to live on the street doesn't mean she..." Murphy halted, seeking the right word... "she's got no *dignity*."

Lucho gave him a dubious glance. "Dignity? What that got to do wit' anythin'?"

Murphy shook his head. "You're an asshole, y'know that?"

Lucho laughed softly. "The chick is hustlin' in the street; *he* talks about dignity, an' *I'm* the asshole?"

"You'll never learn, man. You'll never learn any fucken thing, y'know that? You're just like—"

Suddenly Murphy stopped, his body convulsed by a hacking trill in his chest. He pressed a hand to his mouth, his head bobbing as the spasm forced his lungs. He gagged, riffling in his back pocket, seeking a handkerchief that wasn't there. The hacking became seal-like barks.

Lucho reached in his trousers, extracting a rag which he thrust into Murphy's palm. He watched Murphy stop his mouth with the rag, ejecting sputum into it. "That cough gettin' worse, Pat," he said uneasily.

Murphy lifted his head, and swallowed. "It's nothing," he rasped. "Thing's always been with me." Taking a breath: "It ain't no..."

"The thing gettin' worse, Pat."

Murphy looked him squarely in the eye. "Look, it ain't nothin', okay?"

Lucho started to protest, thought the better of it, and snapped his mouth shut.

Murphy bent down to pick up the trash bags. "Let's get these things out of the way," he urged, getting back his breathing. "It's gettin' late."

"Sure," Lucho said, "anything you say."

## III

GERTIE WENT ACROSS 32ND street and headed into the bowels of Penn Station. Going down the escalator, she gazed intently at the square box she carried, cradling it close to her chest as if it were a newborn babe. With her perennial three bags clumped in her right hand. She went past the subway entrance and into another escalator to the lower level of the promenade, where she found the others at the very end of the walkway. They gathered in a semicircle, passing around a half pint—except for Murphy who placidly smoked a cigarette, but with eyes closed, as if in mediation.

Lula pointed to the box and asked Gertie, "Whatcha got there?"

Gertie didn't say.

Murphy opened his eyes. "Is that from the restaurant where you get the freebees?" he asked.

Gertie bobbed her head up and down in the affirmative.

Lula perused the box with growing interest. "That's a biggie, Gertie. What is it?"

Gertie shrugged her shoulders, her face neutral.

Lucho, leaning on the promenade wall, took a swig from the half pint, passed the bottle to Horse. "Prob'ly grit from that fancy rest'rant in Times Square," he said. "Gertie always get good shit from 'em."

Murphy puffed on his cigarette, then passed it on to Horse, who took a leisurely drag, and said, "Let's see what's inside, Gertie."

"Yeah, it gotta be good," Lula hoped.

Gertie stepped forward and lowered the box to the floor.

Lula shifted forward and lifted the top of the box. "Wow."

Murphy leaned over to look inside. He beamed. "It's a birthday cake—a freakin' birthday cake."

Lucho craned his neck and peered down at the three-layer cake, missing a quarter wedge. The lettering on top stated in bold red: HAPPY BIRTH—

The rest of the word had been cleaved off with the missing wedge. Beneath it were the first four letters of the birthday boy: HOWA—

The rest of Howard's name had gone into someone's stomach. "It's got chocolate layers in between," Lucho observed admiringly.

"A big sucka," Lula added.

Horse whistled slowly. "No jive. That *is* a big sucka. Musta been some big shit for someone."

"Howard knows people and he sure gets around," Murphy judged.

Horse passed the bottle to Lucho, and said, "Looks like we gonna have cake."

Lula grinned. "Shore do." She looked up. "We need somepin to cut it with." She turned to Horse. "Still got yore shiv?"

Horse reached in his back pocket and extracted his knife, handing it to Lula.

Gertie watched as Lula deftly flipped open the blade and began slicing the cake. When she had cut off another wedge she turned to Gertie. "C'mon, Gertie, sit down. You git the first piece."

Gertie formed a lopsided smile.

Lucho took a casual drag on the cigarette, inwardly amazed at how white Gertie's teeth were. Despite all the deprivation, she still retained a semblance of youth.

Murphy tugged at Lucho's arm, and Lucho handed the half-smoked cigarette back to Murphy.

Gertie nestled beside Lula, then took a huge bite of cake, the pastry smearing her lips and chin. Lula chuckled, cutting another piece.

Murphy took the half pint from Horse and downed a big swallow. A feeling of well-being was infused in him. "This is a boon," he said. "Just like a field day back in the crotch."

Lucho devoured a piece of cake. "Whut?" he asked.

Murphy looked up at him. "Y'know. The crotch. Like the service."

"What service?"

"Like the Army, asshole."

Lucho probed his teeth for pieces of cake. "Never heard it called that before."

"That's 'cause you never been in the service."

"Damn tootin'. Too smart for that shit," Lucho said with conviction. "Like da song sez—I is a vet'ran of the war on poverty." He belched, then exhaled slowly. "That's the oney war I know."

"Was you in the war, Murphy?" Lula asked.

Murphy looked down at his hands, did not answer.

Lula went back to the cake, cutting another piece. She handed it to Murphy. "It's good shit," she declared. "Has chocolate filling."

"Fuckin' ay," Horse said in between bites.

Lula touched Gertie's frayed sleeve. "Thank you for sharing the cake with us."

"Yeah, Gertie," Horse added, "you awright. This cake is togetha."

Lula licked a crumb from her pinky finger. "Gertie, you did good. This is one we owe you." She wiped Horse's knife on her jeans, folded the blade back into the handle.

Lucho smacked his lips. "No shit, Gertie. This is okay." He sipped on the wine and gave the bottle to Lula who wiped the spout, then offered to Gertie, "You want some?"

Gertie gaped at the half pint, then back at Lula, shaking her head.

"There's always a first time," Lula proclaimed, tilting back her head and taking a swig.

Murphy said, "Y'know, that's right. I never seen Gertie take a shot." He pointed to the bottle in Lula's hand. "Gertie, you want a shot?"

"Don't knowed," Gertie mumbled.

"Gertie, you ever have a shot of booze?" Lula asked.

"Don't knowed."

"Have a snort," Lucho said. "It'll make ya feel better."

"Don't knowed..."

"Amazing," Murphy said in wonder. "I don't think I ever seen Gertie have a snort."

"That is amazin'," Lula agreed, "'specially hangin' out wit' us."

"Try some," Lucho encouraged. "It'll make ya feel good."

"That it do," Horse said.

"Don't knowed..."

Lula offered the half pint to Gertie. "Heah, take a swig."

"Don't knowed..." Gertie turned to Murphy as if seeking approval.

Murphy nodded. "It's okay, Gertie. You among friends."

Gertie dropped her head to one side, contemplating the half pint in Lula's hand.

Murphy nudged Gertie's elbow. "It's awright."

She reached out tentatively for the bottle. Lula passed it into her hand. Gertie looked around once more, then at the half pint. She brought the bottle to her lips and sucked in lightly. The wine was sweet and fragrant. But she swallowed too fast, and choked.

The rest of them laughed.

Lula took the bottle from her. "You like, Gertie?"

Gertie nodded, her lips spreading into a smile.

Lula held up the half pint in toast. "Happy birthday," she said to all, and followed it with a healthy gulp.

"Well, lookie here," Murphy announced.

Lula glanced down at Murphy. "Say whut?"

Murphy took a drag on his cigarette and pointed, cigarette in hand, toward the promenade area. "Remember him?" he said.

Lula followed Murphy's hand, and she saw the young man who had come to Gertie's aid. "What he doin'?" she asked.

They observed the hard case sifting through the contents inside a large plastic trash can.

Horse clicked his tongue in sympathy. "I'd say he lookin' fer somepin to eat."

"He shore do look homely," Lucho said casually.

"Hey—yo!" Murphy called out.

The others shot him disapproving glances. "Dude's hungry," Murphy told them. He called out again toward the promenade: "Hey, bro!"

The youth lifted his head from inside the trash can. He scanned about, blinking nervously.

"Over here!" Murphy summoned. "Yeah, over here—"

"Whatcha doin', Murphy?" Lula protested. "Leave the asshole alone."

"Yeah, you..."

The youth fixed his eyes on the group surrounding a large open box in the far corner.

"Yeah—*you,* c'mon over."

They saw the young man glance suspiciously to either side of him.

Horse snorted. "What he doin'—casing the joint?"

Murphy waved to the young man. "Hey, man, c'mon over here. Wanna talk to ya."

The young man frowned.

"C'mon, man. Jus' wanna talk to you, that's all."

"Let the fucker go, man," Lucho complained.

Murphy paid no mind, instead motioning for the youth to come over.

The hard case kept his distance.

"C'mon," Murphy urged. "Jus' wanna talk to you." He followed the young man's eyes, which locked onto Gertie's.

Gertie drawled, "Murphy... who he?"

They all stared at her, except for Murphy who said, "You don't remember him from this morning?"

"Nooo..."

"He tried to help you, Gertie," Lula said softly.

"He did?"

Murphy said, "Yes."

Gertie squinted at the slim figure not ten yards away. "Don't 'mem-ber."

"That's okay, Gertie," Murphy said. "I think he awright." He beckoned to the youth. "C'mon, man. C'mon over."

The young man proceeded slowly toward them, stopping three feet from the box. "Whatcha want?" he said, locking eyes with Murphy.

Murphy angled his head toward Gertie. "Wanna thank you for trying to help her this morning."

"Don't need no thanks," the youth said gruffly.

"I know," Lucho reminded. "You said that this morning."

"What's your name?" Murphy asked.

The youth was stolid and unflinching. "Who wants to know?"

"Man, can't you think of somepin else to say every time someone ax yore name?" Horse squawked. "You pissed at the world or somepin?"

The youth scowled. "You wanna make somp'n of it?"

Horse began to rise. But he was checked by Murphy's hand on his elbow. He sat down again as Murphy slowly stood up.

The youth noted Murphy was a head taller than he, and he steeled himself for a fight.

Instead Murphy said carefully, "Look, these are my friends. We hang in together. If you help one of us, we remember." He jerked his thumb toward the box on the floor. "That there is a birthday cake which Gertie here got for us. You was scopin' out the trash, man. You don't hafta do that. You're welcome to share this with us. We only offer once. Like I said, we look out for each other. If you want a piece of cake, you're welcome. If not, then you can slide. We want nuthin' from you, man. We jus' trying to square things, that's all."

The youth eyed the box, then Murphy and the others. Horse scrutinized him with a steady indifference. Lula returned his gaze with a steely reserve. Lucho looked bored. But it was the woman in the overcoat that intrigued him. She showed no reaction at all. Like she was seeing him and not seeing him. Her uneven stare was unsettling.

"What's yore name?" Lucho asked again.

The youth mumbled, "Mario."

"Whut?"

"Mario."

Lula curled her lip slightly. "That's a spic name," she said boldly. "You a spic?"

The youth gave her a caustic look.

"Could be an Italian name," Murphy mused. "But you don't look Italian."

"Yeah, I'm a spic," the youth admitted.

"No probl'm there, slick," Lula wheedled. She leered at Lucho. "He a spic, too. 'Least half of 'im is."

"Yeah," Lucho concurred. "So's Ruben and his ole lady."

Mario looked baffled. "Who?"

"You don't know them yet," Murphy said. He noticed Mario's puzzled glance at Gertie. Murphy smiled, exhibiting his missing front tooth. "This is Gertie, our gopher."

"What?" Lula asked.

"Nothing," Murphy said. "You want some cake?" he asked Mario.

Before the hard case could refuse, Murphy ordered, "Cut 'im a piece."

Lula nonchalantly put out her hand as if holding an invisible tray. Horse brought out his knife, slapping it on Lula's palm. Once more Lula flipped open the blade, never once taking her eyes off Mario. She cut a wedge and handed it to the young man.

Mario cupped the cake gingerly in both hands.

"Sorry we got no napkins," Murphy commented. "It's the maid's night out."

Lucho and Horse looked at each other, smirking.

Once the cake was in hand, all reserve was gone. The youth devoured it in three bites. Crumbs of pastry flecked his chin. He was licking his fingers when suddenly he looked up, noticing the others ogling him. His face hardened again.

"Cut 'im 'nuther piece," Murphy said.

Mario wiped his hands on his pants, and accepted the second piece. "Why don'tcha sit down," Lucho suggested. "Better for the digestion."

Mario tentatively stepped forward, leaning his back on the wall and squatting on the floor. He continued munching on the cake.

"Where you from?" Murphy asked.

Mario stopped chewing. "Around," he answered cautiously.

"Where around?" Horse asked.

Mario probed his upper lip with his tongue. "Jus' around."

"Bet you from the Barrio, man," Lucho guessed.

Mario glanced up at him, not replying.

"Yeah," Lucho continued, "you look like you from the block. Where you from—one hunnert sixteen? Madison Projects? Lexington Projects?"

Horse was puffing on the cigarette which was now down to the filter. He passed it on to Murphy and remarked, "Man is secretive. That's cool. He'll tell us when he wants."

Lula wiped the knife on her blouse sleeve, folded the blade carefully. "We all got secrets," she noted.

Suddenly Murphy stiffened. Lucho felt it. "What up?" he asked.

Murphy nodded in the direction of the concourse. Lucho said, "Oh, man."

Two uniformed policemen were coming their way, followed by a balding, heavyset man. The baldy sweated profusely in a wrinkled summer suit and his tie hung limply from his neck.

"Shit," Lucho cursed. "Here we go again."

"We been through it before," Murphy reminded. "We know what they gonna say."

Lucho groaned. "This is stupid, man. We ain't doin' nuthin'. Why